Praise for the Urgency Emergency! series

★ "Top-notch medical care in an equally terrific early reader that will appeal to preschoolers, new readers of all ages, and anyone else who appreciates droll humor and an inventive plot."
—*Kirkus Reviews*

★ "New readers are in for a treat with these British imports."
—*Horn Book*

"Archer's thickly painted illustrations exude personality and humor, and emerging readers will get a kick out of seeing the repercussions of a familiar story play out in an emergency room setting."—*Publishers Weekly*

"There is plenty of sly humor in the text."—*School Library Journal*

"Valuable lessons about overcoming fears and setting aside differences for others are emphasized…a cute series."—*Library Media Connection*

"The titles could inspire student writing or dramatic projects in a similar vein, while the medical situations are surprisingly educational."—*Bulletin of the Center for Children's Books*, recommended

For Sophie & James

Library of Congress Cataloging-in-Publication Data

Archer, Dosh, author, illustrator.
[Injured spider]
Itsy bitsy spider / Dosh Archer.
pages cm. — (Urgency emergency!)
First published in Great Britain in 2009 under the title: Injured spider.
Summary: "A spider arrives at City Hospital with some strange head injuries. How did this happen? And does it have anything to do with all the water rushing down the water spout?"—Provided by publisher.
[1. Wounds and injuries—Fiction. 2. Medical care—Fiction. 3. Spiders—Fiction. 4. Animals—Fiction. 5. Characters in literature—Fiction. 6. Humorous stories.] I. Title.
PZ7.A6727Its 2013
[E]—dc23
2013005442

Text and illustrations copyright © 2009 by Dosh Archer
First published in Great Britain in 2009 by Bloomsbury Publishing Plc.
Hardcover edition published in 2013 by Albert Whitman & Company
Paperback edition published in 2015 by Albert Whitman & Company
ISBN 978-0-8075-8360-9

Printed in China
10 9 8 7 6 5 4 3 2 1 NP 20 19 18 17 16 15

For more information about Albert Whitman & Company,
visit our web site at www.albertwhitman.com.

URGENCY EMERGENCY!

Itsy Bitsy Spider

Dosh Archer

Albert Whitman & Company
Chicago, Illinois

It was another busy day at City
Hospital. Outside it was pouring
rain. Doctor Glenda was making
an important phone call and Nurse
Percy was looking after one of the
King's men, whose foot had been
squashed by a huge egg.

Just then the
ambulance arrived.

"Urgency Emergency!" called the Pengamedics. "We have an injured spider here. Injured spider coming through!"

Miss Muffet was running beside the trolley. She was the one who had called the ambulance.

"I don't know what happened," cried Miss Muffet. "I was just walking along when I found the spider lying in a puddle of water at the bottom of the waterspout.

I'm afraid of spiders, but I couldn't just leave her lying there."

"Step back!" cried Doctor Glenda.
"Let me examine her."

"It is just as I thought. She is very badly injured. There's a cut on her head. Nurse Percy, put a bandage over that cut to stop any more bleeding."

"Can you tell me your name?" asked Doctor Glenda as she shined a special light into the spider's eyes.
"Itsy Bitsy," said the spider.

"Good," said Doctor Glenda. "How many fingers am I holding up?"

"Two," said Itsy Bitsy.
"That's right," said Doctor
Glenda. "You are in the
hospital because you had
some kind of accident. Can
you tell us what happened?"

"I was just climbing up the waterspout," said Itsy. "Then it started to rain…"

"The last thing I remember is a big whoosh of water rushing toward me."

Doctor Glenda turned to Nurse Percy. "It looks like she was knocked down the waterspout by a downpour of rain. I think her brain is OK, but now we must act quickly—that cut will need stitches."

Itsy trembled with fear. Nurse Percy
put an arm around her.
"Don't worry. It won't hurt a bit."

Nurse Percy gave Itsy a
special injection to stop
the stitches from hurting.

"I will do the stitches myself," said Doctor Glenda.
Nurse Percy brought the special needle and thread.

Very carefully Doctor Glenda made four tiny stitches to hold the cut together so that it could get better.

Nurse Percy held
all of Itsy's hands.

Nurse Percy was right—
it didn't hurt a bit.

Then he put a special sticky
bandage on the cut to keep it nice
and clean so it could heal.

But now Itsy was feeling
a bit wobbly.

"Is there anyone who can help you get home?" asked Nurse Percy.

Itsy shook her head. "My sister is on vacation," she said.

Nurse Percy had an idea.

He went to speak to Miss Muffet.
"I know you are afraid of spiders,"
said Nurse Percy, "but do you think
you could overcome your fears and
look after Itsy just for tonight? She
will be feeling much
better tomorrow."

Miss Muffet looked at poor Itsy.

"Oh, all right," she said. "Come on, Itsy. I don't have any flies for you to eat, but if you don't mind, you can have some of my curds and whey."

"I can never thank you enough," said Itsy Bitsy.

"All in a day's work," said
Doctor Glenda.

Outside the sun had come out
and dried up all the rain. Thanks
to Doctor Glenda and her team,
and with a little help from her
new friend, Miss Muffet, Itsy Bitsy
the spider would soon be climbing
up that waterspout again.

Even more URGENCY EMERGENCY!

COMING SOON!

ISBN 978-0-8075-8356-2